How To Be A Housecat

Written and Illustrated by

Joshua Watts

This book is dedicated to my wife, family, and all
those who have inspired me along the way.
In memory of Gatto

 This book belongs to:

_____

Once there were two cats called Gatto and Poopie. They lived on the second floor of the second flat on the second largest street in the city. Poopie was fat and never shared, whereas Gatto was thin and always got scared. They were both completely different, from claws to fur and paws to purr. But what good housecats they both were.

It was a typical day, and Gatto and Poopie carried out their usual business as they awaited the return of their humans, Camillo and Veronica.

They napped and they scratched...

and they scratched and they sat.

They did nothing unusual for well-behaved housecats. Never did they peep out of the window, nor did they venture onto the balcony, and they absolutely never thought about going outside.

As the day passed by, they couldn't help but feel something strange in the air.

"Shouldn't they be back by now?" Gatto asked.

Poopie huffed, annoyed to be woken up after his fifteenth nap of the day. He looked up at the clock and then in a great panic, he sprang from the sofa.

"They're late! They're never late!" Poopie shouted as he ran to the kitchen, "The bowls are empty; we're going to starve!"

"Oh, I don't like this. I don't like this one bit," Gatto said.

All of a sudden there was a rattling of keys at the door.

"We're home," Veronica said, "and we have a surprise for you!"

The cats rushed to the door and were shocked by what they saw.

"This is Ornella, our new kitten," Camillo said.

The bigger cats were not happy. Poopie hissed like a snake and Gatto leapt onto the bookshelf and began to shake.

"Now you be nice you two, we want you to teach her how to be a good housecat," Veronica said.

But from the moment she arrived, Ornella did everything wrong. She tried to fit in but didn't quite belong.

She ate from their bowls when Poopie hated to share.

She pounced while they slept when she knew Gatto got scared.

She raced and she ripped, and she chased and she tipped.

No matter how hard they tried, Gatto and Poopie just couldn't teach her how to behave.

"You'll never be a housecat," they said.

That night Ornella went to bed quite upset.

"I don't want to be a housecat; I just want to be a ... a ... a cat," she said.

She was just about to close her eyes when all of a sudden something moved outside. It was a black cat, free and wandering around the gardens. Ornella was amazed, and then she had an amazing idea.

"Tomorrow I will be a real cat," she said.

The next morning, Gatto and Poopie were snoozing in their usual spots.

"It's awfully quiet today," Poopie said.
"Where's Ornella?" Gatto asked.
"There she is, over there on the washing line," Poopie said.
"Ok," Gatto replied calmly.

And they both went back to sleep as if the washing line
was a perfectly appropriate place to be for a cat.

A moment later, they startled awake.

"**THE WASHING LINE!**" they both shouted, and they ran to the balcony.
"Ornella get down from there. Housecats don't go outside," Poopie said.
"I am not a housecat!" she said.

Then all of a sudden, the line snapped.

Ornella clung tightly to the line, and before she knew it, she was swinging into the neighbour's garden.

"What do we do?"
Gatto said with a trembling voice.

"There's nothing we can do.
Housecats don't go outside!"
Poopie said.

"We have to bring her back,"
Gatto said, climbing onto the drainpipe.

"You can't go down there.
You're a scaredy cat," Poopie said.

But for a moment, Gatto forgot his fears,
slid down the drainpipe and
climbed into the neighbour's garden.

Poopie was shocked.
But he couldn't let Gatto go on alone,
so he struggled down the drainpipe
and hopped over the wall.

They searched and they followed Ornella,
but she was always one step ahead.

She hopped the fence and played with a
frog,

whilst they were pecked by hens
and chased by the dog.

She found a man who sang to his crop,
whilst they were cursed and shooed away
with a mop.

She ran through the grass
to catch a mouse,
whilst they got tangled and twisted
and longed for the house.

She leapt with joy and never felt more alive.

"Ornella, stop!" they said, "get back inside."

Up, up and up she scaled the church wall.
She sat by the bells and could see all.

"Ornella!" They shouted with a huff and a puff,
"We've chased you all day, and enough is enough."

They sat down beside her to catch their breath.

"I'm sorry, but I don't want to be a housecat. I want to be free," she said.

But Gatto and Poopie didn't reply. Instead, they stared out into the distance, and it was the furthest they had ever seen.

"Never in all my years have I ever felt more... alive," Poopie said.

"What?" Ornella replied.

"He's right, and I don't feel as scared," Gatto said.

"But what about being a housecat?" she said.

"Oh, there's plenty of time for that. But thank you for teaching us how to be a cat," Poopie said.

They stayed a little longer until Ornella fell asleep. Poopie picked her up, and they made their way home through the grass, over the walls and back up the drainpipe to the second floor.

Poopie placed her in his big bed, finally learning how to share.

Some days they went for an adventure, and others they stayed inside, and all was good at number two ...

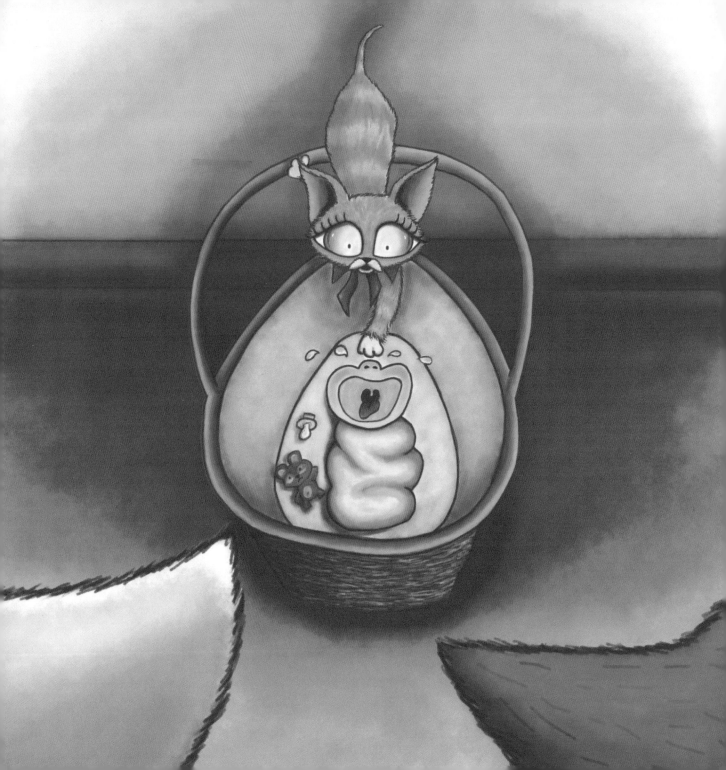

Until Camillo and Veronica brought home
another surprise.

The end.

Stay tuned for more books and creations...

If you'd like to support me and follow my journey as an independent author please follow me at:

 jwattsdaydreams

jwattsdaydreams